The Magic Door Series

BOOK 1

The Moon Robber

By Dean Morrissey and Stephen Krensky
Pictures by Dean Morrissey

HarperCollins*Publishers*

For Carl and Lorraine Layman
—D.M.

For Andrew and Peter
—S.K.

Library of Congress Cataloging-in-Publication Data
Morrissey, Dean.
The moon robber / by Dean Morrissey and Stephen Krensky ; pictures by
Dean Morrissey.
p.   cm.
Summary: Joey, Michael, and Sarah pass through a magic door into the land of Great
Kettles, where they help recover the moon from a giant who had stolen it.
ISBN 0-06-028581-8 — ISBN 0-06-028582-6 (lib. bdg.)
[1. Moon—Fiction.]   I. Krensky, Stephen.   II. Title.
PZ7.M84532 Mo   2001   00-33586
[Fic]—dc21

Typography by Stephanie Bart-Horvath
1   2   3   4   5   6   7   8   9   10
❖
First Edition

CHAPTER ONE

"Is that really true?" asked Joey. He was holding a forked stick in one hand. A rubber band was stretched across the ends.

Two other children, Sarah and Michael, were standing at the window of the Magic Door Toyshop. Michael was ten, the same as Sarah. Joey was only six.

"Hey," said Michael, "I wouldn't make that up."

Sarah just laughed.

Joey did not look convinced. "Well, maybe . . ."

"Maybe what?" said Sam, returning from the back room. He was the owner of the shop as well as its chief toy maker.

Joey held up the stick. "Michael says that this toy is for finding water underground. Is that right?"

Sam often played a game with the children. He would set a toy on his workbench and let them guess what it was. The toys were made of wood or cloth,

filled with stuffing, and decorated with buttons or
paint. They weren't like the toys the children usually
played with.

"Don't listen to Michael, Joey," said Sarah. "He's
just teasing. You're holding a slingshot. My dad has
one from the old days. I've tried it a couple of times."

"Absolutely right, Sarah," said Sam, taking it back
from Joey. "Slingshots have been around for thousands
of years. They were originally used by hunters to knock
out small animals."

"Did you play with one when you were a boy?" Joey asked.

Sam smiled. "Sometimes. We would aim at targets. But I never used one on this side of the magic door."

He was referring to a door in one of the walls. It had an arched top and a great rusted bolt and latch.

The children had never seen the door open. There was no room behind it, and they thought of the door as a decoration, one that had given Sam the name for his shop.

"Of course," Sam added, "some toys are still—"

Suddenly, a strange rumble passed all around them—as though the whole shop had suddenly sneezed.

"Look!" cried Joey.

He pointed to the middle of the table. The gumball machine had started to shake like some kind of musical instrument.

More things began to shake.

"What is it?" cried Sarah. "An earthquake?"

"In Old Bridgeport?" said Michael. "We've never had one before."

Sam dropped the slingshot into his apron pocket. "Outside, quick! An earthquake could level the shop."

They rushed into the street, expecting to find it filled with people. But the street was quiet, and the rumbling was gone. There was no broken glass or heaving cobblestones.

Sarah blinked. "I don't get it."

Sam was frowning. Cautiously, he stuck his head back in the shop.

The children poked their heads in around him.

"Is it safe yet?" asked Michael.

Sam looked around. The room was now perfectly still. "I suppose so. But stay on your toes."

"I've never heard of an inside-only earthquake," said Sarah.

"I'm not sure it was an earthquake," said Sam. "I'm going to check for damage upstairs. You three stay here."

The children began picking up some of the fallen toys.

"That was my first earthquake," said Joey, beaming.

"Mine too," said Sarah.

"Maybe," said Michael, "if that's what it really was." He stopped talking, staring at the wall behind the workbench.

There, right before his eyes, the magic door was open.

CHAPTER TWO

"Wow!" cried Joey.

He ran forward, opening up the door for a better look.

The opening in front of him did not lead outside to the harbor that he knew lay on the other side of the wall. Instead, it opened into a dusty shop.

Michael looked surprised. "But there's no shop next to this one."

"And there's no door on the outside wall, either," added Sarah.

Neither of these facts made the other shop look any less real.

"Look!" said Joey. "It's the clock tower."

He pointed to a distant

shape visible through the other shop's windows.

Michael squinted. "What clock tower? There's no clock tower in Old Bridgeport."

"Not here—the one I told you about before, the one in the Great Kettles."

Sarah's mouth dropped. "You mean the place where you said you went in that time machine?"

Joey nodded.

Sarah and Michael had both heard Joey's story. According to him, the Great Kettles was a group of islands across the Sea of Time. Among the characters who lived there were the Sandman and Father Time. Sarah and Michael had really never been sure how much of the story was true—and how much had come out of Joey's imagination.

But here was the proof, right in front of their eyes.

"This is great!" said Joey. "I always wanted to go back."

Before anyone could stop him, Joey stepped forward—and jumped into the shop.

"Joey, you come back here this instant!" Sarah ordered.

But Joey just ignored her, running off out of sight.

Sarah and Michael looked at each other.

"We can't leave him there all alone," she said.

"Besides, we'll come right back," he said.

The next second they too had passed through the doorway. The shop was dusty and seemed deserted, as though no one had been there in a long time. But it was not empty. Along the shelves were all kinds of different toys.

"Unbelievable!" said Michael, turning around slowly.

"It's the same as Sam's shop only backward," Sarah said. "Like a mirror."

Joey popped out from behind one of the counters. "What took you so long?" he said. "I've been waiting forever."

Sarah frowned. "What do you mean? We came right after you."

"Oh no," said Joey. "It's been awhile. But I remember from before—time doesn't work the same in the Great Kettles. It goes faster here."

Michael didn't like the sound of that. "Maybe we should go back," he said slowly.

"Not yet," said Joey. "You just got here."

Knock, knock.

The children looked out the shop windows. An

old woman carrying a basket of onions stood outside peering in at them.

"Hide," said Joey.

"We can't hide," said Michael. "She's already seen us."

Sarah walked to the front door and opened it.

"What are you children doing here?" the woman demanded. Her skin was wrinkled and leathery, but her eyes were as bright as stars. "You surprised me. This shop has been empty for a very long time. And I should know. Not much gets by Videlia Potts, the Onion Lady."

"Pleased to meet you, Miss Potts. I'm Sarah. This is Michael and Joey."

"Hello," the two boys said together.

"You look like you've lost your way," Miss Potts observed. "It's clear enough you're not from the Kettles." She looked them over. "Came through that magic door, I expect."

"You know about the magic door?" said Joey.

She smiled. "You don't get to be my age without learning a few things. The magic doors are connections between here and the Outland. But our lives are bound together in many other ways as well."

"That sounds like a lot of fairy-tale stuff," said Michael. "It's not real."

"Then, it might be best to leave it that way. Why don't you turn around and go back home? Just chalk this up to a daydream. Besides, this really isn't a very safe place just now." Her eyes searched the sky out the window.

"No, no," Sarah put in quickly. "Don't listen to him, Miss Potts. He's just being stubborn. I believe you. In fact, now that we're here, we'd like— whoa!"

The ground beneath them began to shake, sending them staggering across the floor.

"Earthquake!" cried Joey. "Run for your lives!"

CHAPTER THREE

But before Joey, or anyone else, had a chance to move, the earthquake stopped.

"Funny kind of earthquake," said Sarah.

Michael shook his head. "Can't make up its mind if it's starting or not," he said.

"It wasn't an earthquake, my dears," said Miss Potts.

"No?" said Michael. "What else can make the ground shake that much?"

"Oh, goodness," said the Onion Lady, "any number of things. But in this case, there's no mystery about it. Mogg was responsible."

"Mogg?" said Sarah. "What's Mogg?"

"Mogg isn't a *what*, dear, he's a *who*. A giant, to be more precise."

"A giant?" said Michael. "A real giant?"

Videlia Potts frowned. "Naturally. We don't have

much call for fake giants in the Great Kettles."

"How big a giant?" asked Michael.

Miss Potts stopped to think. "Well, Mogg is the only giant I know. But he's certainly taller than most of the trees hereabouts."

Sarah let out a deep breath. "That's a giant, all right."

"Bold as brass he was too. Came through town about an hour ago. Emptied most of my kettle of soup at one swallow. I was making a big batch for the festival. 'Goes down easy,' he bellowed, 'like a sword through a feather bed.' That's the way Mogg talks. He fancies himself a pirate, you see. Lives on Fish Island, dragging up bits of old ships he finds off the shore." She paused. "But I don't believe he was really after the soup. He seemed to be looking for something else."

"Do you think he'll come back?" Joey asked hopefully.

"Hard to say. Giants are not very predictable."

"Well, I want to go out and look around."

"Yes," said Michael. "It would be something to see a giant."

"But, Michael," said Miss Potts, "you can't actually

believe in giants. After all, aren't they in fairy tales too?"

Michael wasn't sure what to say.

Joey took a deep breath. "Let's go!"

He led the way out into the street. Sarah followed him straightaway, but Michael hesitated a moment.

"Well," he said slowly, "any scientist knows it's good to keep an open mind."

"Fair enough," said Miss Potts, smiling.

Michael smiled back, and then he ran to catch up with the others.

He found them in the village square, staring at a carriage pulled by a checkered horse. A stately stone building with slate roof and arched windows stood next to a shop shaped like a huge stovepipe hat. There was a bakery and a general store.

The people going about their business were not dressed in modern clothes, Sarah noted, but were wearing what she thought of as old-fashioned costumes.

"Welcome to Moonhaven," said Miss Potts behind them.

"It's like walking into a play," whispered Michael.

One of the passersby, a farmer, was leading a cow past them. It was a black cow with gold stars in its

coat. Every now and then, the cow would give a little leap and float into the air.

"Just practicing," the farmer told them. "Nothing to be alarmed about."

"I know that cow," said Joey. "That's the cow that jumps over the moon."

"But that's not possible," Michael began. "Oh, never mind."

"And that's the moon itself," Joey added.

He was pointing to a large round machine sitting on a wooden platform.

Sarah frowned. "The moon? But it looks like a flying machine."

"And it has a face on the front," said Michael. "I've never seen the moon with a face."

"Well, you've never been this *close* before," Miss Potts reminded him. "Things don't always look the same at a distance."

"You're saying this is our moon?" said Sarah. "The one we see in our sky?"

"The one and only," said Miss Potts. "Of course, the moon doesn't always look the same. The Man in the

Moon, Captain Luna, lights it differently depending on the time of month."

"The Man in the Moon?" said Sarah. "There really is such a person?"

"Of course. He brings the moon to your world every night."

Michael folded his arms. "Could we meet him?" he asked.

Miss Potts considered it. "He's probably inside,

tinkering with the machinery. But I should warn you, the captain can be cranky—especially if his machinery is not behaving."

"And how often is that?" asked Michael.

Miss Potts smiled. "Almost always," she admitted.

"Knock again, Sarah," said Joey.

The three children were standing at a door outside the moon's entryway. The sound of muffled clanking and the grinding of gears came from inside.

Knock, knock.

Sarah frowned. "I don't think he can hear us."

"Then let's go find him," said Joey.

They opened the door and climbed inside. There they found a staircase that spiraled upward along the moon's outer hull. The children walked up and up and up, finally reaching a small windowed compartment.

"This must be the control room," said Sarah.

The leather-paneled walls smelled of oil and dust. Brass levers and handles hung overhead, and wires ran in every direction. And right before them was a panel covered with dials and switches.

"This still doesn't look like the moon to me," Michael insisted.

Above them was an open hatch. It seemed to lead out to the rest of the structure.

"Helllooooo!" Joey shouted.

There was no answer.

Michael was studying the control panel. "I do recognize these dials. I've seen this kind of thing in old books." He tapped one of the crystal covers. "This one measures altitude. The next is wind speed."

"What about this one?" asked Sarah, pulling on a shiny lever directly overhead.

The compartment suddenly lurched to one side.

"Sarah, what did you do?" Michael demanded.

"Nothing. I might have pulled this lever . . . a little."

"Well, unpull it," Michael ordered. "And quickly!"

"Too late," said Joey, pointing out the window.

The moon had already slipped its mooring. As the children looked out in horror, they rose quickly into the sky.

CHAPTER FOUR

Sarah and Michael joined Joey at the window. Below them the trees and houses were getting smaller and smaller.

"At least we're not rising too fast," said Sarah.

"The moon never rises fast," Joey reminded her.

"There's a reason for that," said a voice from the hatch above them. "Not that you're entitled to any explanations."

A short man in a full-dress uniform descended the ladder. His coat had brass buttons and checkered lapels.

"I'm sorry," said Sarah. "It was my fault. But maybe you should have posted warning signs."

"Warning signs? *Warning signs!* Young lady, I don't need warning signs. I'm the only one who's supposed to work the controls."

He brushed past her and examined the dials.

"Nothing broken, at least. Stand back! Stand back, I say!"

"Who is he?" Sarah whispered to Joey.

"He's the Man in the Moon," Joey answered. "Captain Luna. We've met before."

The captain gave Joey a closer look. "Hmmm . . . You do appear vaguely familiar."

"This is quite a machine," Michael admitted. "But I don't see how it could be the moon."

"No, I suppose you don't," said the captain. "But

perhaps you were dropped on your head as a baby. In any event, that's not my problem." He looked at them darkly. "But you are. The question is, what should I do about you? You don't belong here."

"We could stand by quietly," said Michael, "and watch you work."

"Very quietly," said Sarah.

"Like mice," Joey added.

"I don't allow mice on my vessel," the captain pointed out.

"Hellloooooooo! Anybody home?"

These words came from somewhere outside, sending all three children scurrying to the window. There, bobbing on a wave of clouds, was a quilted tugboat. Sitting at the stern was a tall man wearing a wispy white robe.

A stack of what looked like burlap bags were sitting at the man's side. He was filling the bags from a steam pump.

"Go away!" the captain shouted.

The man on the ship sighed. "You don't mean that."

"Indeed I do!"

"Captain, let's speak frankly. This ship of yours is a disgrace, the most dreadfully dreary scow in the sky.

And here I am, offering to dress it up a bit. So, what do you say? Let's give this tattered tub a little makeover."

"What!" the captain shouted. "You get in here and I'll give you a makeover."

"I thought you'd never ask," said the man. A moment later, the door opened and he drifted inside.

"Oh, my," he said. "I didn't know you had company." He bowed to the children. "Skylar T. Peddlefogg at your service. I am the cloud keeper."

Captain Luna folded his arms. "State your business, Peddlefogg—and be gone!"

"Have it your own way," said the cloud keeper, winking at the children. "I never argue with a customer, especially a cranky one."

"I am not a customer!"

"I don't understand," said Joey.

Peddlefogg nodded. "Let me explain," he said. "The problem is the moon. It's a technological marvel, to be sure, but still somewhat lacking a certain, well, dignity."

"Peddlefogg wants to sell me a cloud," Captain Luna explained.

"Clouds are for sale?" said Michael.

"Have you ever bought one?" asked Sarah.

"Once," the captain admitted. "But only once. The cloud didn't last very long—and he wouldn't take it back. Told me the warranty had expired."

The cloud keeper waved his arm. "Let's not dwell on the past. I represent a whole new line of clouds now. The samples lie out the window there."

"Bah!" muttered the captain. "I'll never get any work done with all these interruptions. Very well, if it will get you to leave, I'll take one."

"May I recommend the Rainy Day Linen Plump?"

"Nothing so fancy," said the captain. "Give me a Number Six Cotton Drifter. You can attach it just under the door."

"The Number Six," said Peddlefogg, sighing. "A frugal choice. It's delicate, you know. Easily punctured."

"Are you try-ing to talk me out of it?"

"Not at all," the cloud keeper said quickly. "The Number Six it is. You won't regret it, I promise you."

Captain Luna grunted and handed over a few small coins. "I'm regretting it already."

Peddlefogg ignored this last remark. With his sale complete, he smiled at the children and left.

The children watched through the window as he attached the little cloud to the side of the moon.

"How does he do that?" asked Michael, watching the cloud keeper sail away. "Stay up like that, I mean."

"Is it kind of like a magic carpet?" asked Joey.

"I'm not familiar with such things," said the captain. "And I don't want to become— whoa!"

The whole moon shook for a moment. Then it grew still.

Michael and Joey turned to Sarah.

"What did you do now?" they asked together.

Sarah held up her hands. "Nothing," she said. "Honest."

"The propeller's stopped," said the captain, frowning. "But we haven't run into anything." He pulled at several levers in turn. None of them would budge.

"What happens when the propeller stops?" asked Sarah.

"We fall," the captain said simply.

"But we're not falling, are we?" asked Michael.

"No," the captain admitted, "and that's very odd. We— hold on!"

The moon shook again.

"We may not be falling," said Michael. "But we are going down."

Joey looked out the window. "It's the giant!" he cried.

Michael and Sarah rushed to the side.

"Look at his fingers!" said Sarah. "They're as big as tree trunks."

"And as strong as them, too," Michael noted. "He just reached up and grabbed us."

They were right. Mogg had plucked them right out of the sky. Now he was pulling them down to rest on his shoulder.

"What do we do?" asked Michael.

"Confounded nuisance," muttered the captain.

"But you have a plan, don't you?" asked Sarah.

"No!" snapped the Man in the Moon. "I don't."

CHAPTER FIVE

Michael had turned a little green.

"Like a lily pad," Joey said admiringly.

"I've never been good on roller coasters," Michael murmured, "and this is much worse."

"W-we have to do something," said Sarah. "Fire the retro rockets! Blast our way free!"

"The moon is not equipped with such devices," said the captain.

"Well, then, could we drop something on the giant's head?"

"That might not be wise," reported the captain, pointing out the window.

The children looked, too—and saw only the land far below.

Sarah frowned. "Well, I'm sure we can think of something."

But try as she might, Sarah couldn't come up with

a plan. She realized she lacked experience in situations where she was trapped inside the moon while being kidnapped by a giant.

Suddenly, they came to a halt.

"We've stopped!" said Joey.

Sarah staggered over to the window. "Joey's right," she said. "He's set us back down."

Michael didn't say a word, but he had never been gladder of anything in his life.

"I wonder where we are," said Sarah. "Wait! What is *that*?"

A strange winged animal flew by the window. It had the face and body of a large rabbit, but with broad, feathered wings stretching out of each side.

"That's a gullhare," said Captain Luna. "And this is Fish Island. It's where Mogg lives. The gullhares are harmless. They eat seaweed and grass. Mogg, I'm not so sure about."

"Why, what will he do to us?" asked Michael, who had started to feel better.

Captain Luna examined his instrument panel. "I, for one, have no wish to stick around and find out. We're leaving!"

He grabbed a lever above his head and pulled hard.

A grinding noise filled the air.

"That's trouble," he said, sighing. "Sounds like a transfer gear." He tapped on the dials.

"Why did Mogg grab us, anyway?" asked Sarah.

Michael took a deep breath. His color was slowly returning to normal. "Miss Potts did say he was looking for something. Maybe it was the moon."

"But why would he want the moon?" Joey asked. "And what will he do with it?"

"Or us?" added Michael.

Nobody knew.

Michael took a look out the window. There didn't seem to be anyone, big or small, around. "Does Mogg know how the moon works?" he asked.

Captain Luna was inspecting his machinery. "No reason he should," he muttered.

"So Mogg might not know we're aboard."

"Anything's possible," said the captain. He opened the hatch.

"Where are you going?" asked Sarah.

"To inspect the damage."

"Can we come too?" asked Joey.

"What you do or don't do is hardly my concern. At least as long as you *stay out of my way.*"

The children followed him out.

"Well, that tears it!" muttered the captain, from the bottom of the ladder.

One of the large propeller blades had been jarred loose.

"Can you fix it?" asked Michael.

Captain Luna frowned. "I'm not a miracle worker. But we'll see."

"Look at that!" said Joey, staring up the hill.

He pointed to a huge lantern.

"AAAACCCCHHHHHHHHH!"

The unexpected rumbling echoed all around them.

"Where is it coming from?" asked Sarah.

"Let's find out," said Joey. "Do you want to come, Captain?"

"I'm not here to see the sights. You run along."

The children started down a path that led through a grove of trees. The rumbling got louder.

At the top of a stony hill, they stopped.

In the vale below, Mogg lay on the ground, snoring. He was stretched out like a mountain of rumpled laundry. He had on a striped cap, a puffy white shirt, a red and green vest with brass buttons, and maroon leggings.

"AAAACCCCCHHHHHHHHHH!"

"Miss Potts was right," said Sarah. "He does look like a pirate."

"A snoring pirate," Joey whispered.

Tiptoeing around the slumbering Mogg, the children entered a walled courtyard. It was filled with objects—great chests, broken masts, and rusty anchors.

"Treasure!" cried Joey.

"Look at the seaweed and dried salt on these things," said Michael. "I think Mogg pulled this stuff off the beach or from under the water."

Suddenly, they heard another noise. But this was not a rumble.

"What's that?" whispered Joey.

Beyond the courtyard, a vast shadow was sweeping across the ground.

"Whatever it is," said Michael, "we can't go back. I think Mogg is waking up."

The others nodded—and pressed on ahead.

CHAPTER SIX

Joey, Sarah, and Michael stood staring with their mouths open.

High above their heads, the arms of an old windmill shuddered in the breeze. It had four long arms, each one covered with sailcloth. Behind the arms sat a squat tower with a flat top. There was a door at the front under a small window. Some of the panes in the window were broken.

The creaking arms were making all the noise.

"I thought windmills went around and around," said Sarah.

"They do," said Michael. "This one must be broken."

Joey scrambled up to the door and pushed it open. Inside there was a lot of dust and cobwebs.

"Wow, this is great!" he exclaimed, disturbing the rats, which scurried out of sight.

Sarah and Michael waved away some cobwebs as they entered behind him.

Joey ran up to some wooden gears. "How do these work?" he asked.

"Windmills are an old source of power," said Michael. "They're used to mill grain or move water or generate electricity."

"Does it work?" Joey asked.

"Maybe," said Michael. "The movement of the blades is controlled by the gears. We could free them by"—he traced a finger along the ropes and pulleys—"releasing the lock."

He pulled down on the last rope, releasing the brake from the main gear.

Without warning, the windmill shrieked mournfully to life.

Sarah put her hands over her ears. "It sounds like fingernails on a blackboard. Make it stop!"

"No way," said Michael, feeling very pleased with himself. "Who knows how long this thing would have sat here if I hadn't come along?"

As something blocked the light from the window, Sarah looked up slowly. "Uh-oh," she said.

"Double uh-oh," Michael added.

Mogg towered above them, scratching his head and yawning. He wasn't thinking very clearly, and he didn't understand why the windmill had started spinning. He bent down to take a look inside.

"Thieves!" Mogg roared.

He reached down to grab them, disturbing a flock of gullhares nestling in the rocks. They flapped upward, startling Mogg and making him fall back.

"Stupid birds!" he cried. "Shoo! Shoo!"

"Run!" cried Sarah. "Quickly!"

They scrambled out the door and down the path. Mogg was too big to outrun on open ground, but maybe they could hide among the trees.

"Thieves!" Mogg shouted again.

"I don't think he likes us!" said Joey.

"You're just figuring that out?" said Michael.

They kept on running. They could hear Mogg spreading apart the canopy of branches, but that slowed him down enough for the children to stay ahead.

"If we could get back to the moon," said Michael, "we could hide inside. He doesn't know it opens up."

"Maybe he'll forget about us after a while," said Joey. "You know, he could be like a dinosaur. Big, but with a tiny brain."

"Thieves! Thieves!" Mogg was still crashing through the trees.

"He's not giving up," said Michael.

They broke into a clearing and scrambled over the rocks. The moon was only a short dash away.

"We'll be safe soon," said Sarah.

KA-BOOM!

A small explosion went off somewhere inside the moon. A few seconds later, Captain Luna burst from the hatch, coughing.

The children rushed over to his side.

"Well, that didn't go well," he muttered. "I thought I could free up the propeller blade." He looked back at the smoldering moon. "It appears I was mistaken."

"Captain, I see you haven't changed a bit," said an unexpected voice behind them.

CHAPTER SEVEN

It was Sam.

"Hooray!" cried Joey.

Sarah and Michael ran up to him at once.

Sam gave them each a hug. "I'm so glad you're safe. When I realized you'd gone through the magic door, I was flabbergasted. That door had been rusted shut for . . . well, let's just say a very long time. I followed you through straightaway, but with the time difference, you had already left on the moon."

"But how did you know we were here?" asked Sarah.

Sam laughed. "Videlia—Miss Potts—told me. It wasn't exactly a secret. When Mogg grabbed you out of the sky, anyone within a few miles had a fine view. After that, I borrowed a boat and sailed here to his home as fast as I could."

"Now that you've come," said Joey, "we'll show

that giant he can't push us around. What did you bring with you?"

"Actually," said Sam, "I didn't bring anything— well, other than whatever I had in my pockets." He felt around and brought out the slingshot.

Sarah took it from him and picked up a stone from the ground. "This would be like David and Goliath," she said.

"Except that Goliath wasn't this big," said Sam. He turned to Captain Luna. "How are you, Horatio? It's been a long time."

The captain shrugged. "I haven't been keeping track."

"You two know each other?" asked Sarah.

"Oh, yes," said Sam.

He stopped talking because Mogg had just appeared over the ridge. The giant had heard the explosion and had hurried to investigate.

"Hide!" cried Sam.

But there was nowhere to go. Mogg was on them in three steps.

"More thieves!" he cried.

Thinking quickly, Sam scrambled up on a bluff to address the giant. "You insult me with your

accusations, Large Sir. If we were thieves, we would be carting away spoils. As you can see for yourself, we carry nothing. We are, in fact, a traveling troupe of, um, magicians. Magicians of the most powerful sort. And you would be well advised—very well advised— to leave us be."

Hands on hips, Sam stared at the giant during a long, uncomfortable silence.

Suddenly, the giant burst into laughter. "A magician . . ." he finally uttered, wiping tears from his eyes. "That's really good." He dropped abruptly to his knees and faced Sam with a scowl. "Well, Magician, show me your magic wand."

"My wand? Ah, yes, my wand . . ." Sam hesitated.

"That's right," said Mogg. "Every magician has a wand."

"I have it here!" Sarah said suddenly, holding up the slingshot.

Mogg folded his arms. "I have never seen such a wand before. Now show me some magic."

While Sam had been speaking, Michael had been looking around for something that would help them out. His eye settled on the cloud—and his face brightened.

"Sarah," he whispered, "remember what the cloud keeper said."

Sarah looked blankly for a moment. Then her face broke into a smile. She cradled the stone in the sling and pulled it back.

Joey said nothing, but his eyes couldn't open any wider. What was Sarah thinking? Her shot would bother Mogg no more than a mosquito bite.

But Sarah wasn't aiming at the giant. She shot at the Number Six Cotton Drifter.

The stone whizzed through the air, puncturing the cloud.

"Fog!" cried Joey.

Fog, indeed. It poured out of the cloud like smoke from a chimney. It swirled around Mogg's feet. He lifted his feet to stamp it out, but while his blows shook the ground, the fog continued to grow.

The fog billowed upward, enveloping the giant in a wet mist.

"Cotton drifters never were very sturdy," said Sam. "Now it's time to disappear." The fog was thinnest close to the ground, and Sam led them quickly away while Mogg stomped around blindly nearby.

CHAPTER EIGHT

Sam led the others to a rocky cove where his sailboat was hidden. A giant lantern lay to one side, resting on an outcropping.

"We're safe for the moment," he said. "We'll go back after dark."

"Back?" said Michael.

"We can't leave the moon where it is," Sam explained. "It's much more than a light crossing the night sky. The moon regulates the ocean tides both here and in the Outland. Why, without it there'd be floods, tidal waves—"

"All manner of watery calamities," Captain Luna finished for him.

Sam took a basket out of the boat. "But we may as well be comfortable while we wait," he said cheerfully. "I've got bread, cheese, and fruit—all courtesy of Miss Potts."

The children had forgotten about eating, but their appetites came back in a hurry. Even the captain accepted the food without protest.

"By the way, Sarah," said Sam, "how did you know the cloud would leak out as fog?"

"I didn't. It was Michael's idea, really."

"Oh?"

"I remembered what Mr. Peddlefogg said about them," Michael explained. "I was hoping the cloud would explode or something."

"But how can one cloud make so much fog?" Joey asked.

"It's a question of pressure," Captain Luna put in. "The inside is compressed so that the cloud will last a

long time. It was quick thinking, children, I'll grant you that."

"I understand Mogg grabbed the moon right out of the sky," said Sam. "Has he ever tried to do that before?"

"No," the captain admitted.

"I wonder why he started now. He must have had a reason."

Nobody was ready to take the chance and ask.

At dusk, the stars began coming out, and Sarah noticed that they looked bigger and brighter than the stars at home.

"Are we closer to the stars here?" she asked Sam.

"Actually, we're almost among them. You can't quite see it from the island, but we're not far from the mill where the Sandman makes the stars."

"If you two are done gabbing," said the captain, "there's work to be done. I want to complete my repairs so we can be on our way before Mogg knows what happened."

"ARRRGGHHH!"

The growl seemed to echo all around them.

Sam motioned the children to crouch down.

"What's that noise?" Joey whispered.

"The wind, I hope," said Michael.

"Give it to me, I say!"

"I think it's the giant," said Sarah. "It sounds like he's talking to someone."

"ARRRRGGGGHHHH!"

Michael blinked. "He doesn't sound too happy," he said.

"Maybe he has someone else trapped," said Joey.

"Or it could be a trick," said Michael.

"AAARRRRRRRGGGGGGGGHHHH!"

Sam rubbed his chin. "Perhaps we should take a look."

They climbed back up the slope, past the windmill and onto the path through the courtyard.

Even in the dark, it was easy to pick out Mogg sitting on the edge of a cliff.

"What's that he's holding?" Sarah whispered.

"The moon!" said Michael.

Mogg moaned again. "Where is your light?" he asked. "Why won't you light?"

Mogg shook the moon a little, but that didn't make the light come on, either.

"What does he think he's doing?" hissed the captain. "That's a delicate piece of machinery."

"Ssssssh!" said Sam.

Mogg poked at the moon uselessly.

Sam stepped forward for a better look and accidentally snapped a twig under his foot.

Craaccck!

Mogg spun around toward the sound. "Who's there?" he asked.

Everyone froze. After a long while, Mogg turned his attention back to the moon.

"He sure sounds different than he did this afternoon," said Sarah.

"He's afraid," said Joey.

The others all stared at him.

"How can you know that?" asked Michael.

"I just do."

Sarah snorted. "Joey, are you saying what I think you're saying?"

Joey nodded. "Mogg," he said, "is afraid of the dark."

CHAPTER NINE

"Absolutely not."

"I think you should reconsider," said Sam.

"I don't have to reconsider," the captain insisted. "My mind is made up."

They had been arguing like that for some time.

"We need to fix this problem," Sam said yet again. "Otherwise, even if you get the moon back, Mogg may try to steal it again. Besides, I know you can spare the parts. You have more back in your workshop."

The captain would not budge. "My ship and what I can spare from her are not your concern. There is nothing you can say that—"

"Do you hear me, moon?" Mogg shouted. "If you do not light, I will throw you into the ocean."

The captain gasped.

"I'm beginning to see your point," he said hastily.

"Hurry up, before he does something foolish."

Sam walked forward until he was close enough for Mogg to hear him, but not so close that he couldn't retreat quickly if necessary.

"Mogg!"

The giant looked up. "Who's there?"

"It's Sam Thacher. The, uh, magician from this afternoon."

Mogg began waving his arms. There wasn't any fog in sight, but he was taking no chances.

"I remember," he said.

"We want to help you," Sam went on.

"Help how?" asked Mogg.

"You took the moon because it is a bright light. Correct?"

"It is not bright now," the giant pointed out. "It does not work."

"But you wish it did."

Mogg nodded. "I had a lantern. A magic lantern. I still have it. But it no longer works. The magic is gone."

"A lantern like that must have cast a strong light," Sam continued. "Without it, things around here must get pretty dark."

Mogg stared at the ground. "Some nights the moon is bright, but not always. If the moon stays here, the light will be enough."

"But other people need the moon too," Sam reminded him.

Mogg looked a little embarrassed. "Other people have friends and family."

"That's not the point," Captain Luna declared. He had crept forward quietly during Sam's conversation, but he could remain silent no longer.

"Who is that?" asked Mogg.

"It is I, Captain Horatio Luna, the Man in the Moon. Put down my ship this instant."

"Your ship?" Mogg sounded confused. "You travel inside the moon?"

"Naturally."

"I didn't know," said Mogg.

Captain Luna snorted. "I suppose you thought the moon just sailed across the sky by itself?"

Mogg was silent.

The captain threw up his hands. "Typical. Why should I be

surprised? My work is never appreciated. Do you realize how difficult it is to keep the moon aloft? No, of course you don't."

"The point," Sam said quickly, "is that the moon must be shared. But cheer up, Mogg. With your help and our magic, we can solve your problem. Release the moon—and we'll put a light in your lantern that will never go out. Do we have a deal?"

Mogg thought it over. "Yes," he said finally. "Can I help?"

"Of course," Sam assured him. "The truth is, we can't do it without you."

Mogg stood up. "Then what are we waiting for?"

"My sentiments exactly!" said the captain. "Follow me, Mogg!" he ordered, marching off toward the windmill. "And whatever you do, watch your step!"

Under the captain's direction, the work went quickly. Sam and the children carried supplies from inside the moon over to the windmill. Mogg then placed his old lantern on top of it.

The captain then removed one generator and the starboard lantern bank from the moon. Mogg carried them over to the windmill.

Meanwhile, Sarah, Michael, and Joey ran wires

from the lantern base down inside the windmill itself.

"Make sure the wires are twisted tightly," said Michael.

"Check!" said Sarah.

"Are the connections wrapped in tape?"

"Check!" said Joey.

When the generator was connected to the windmill's main shaft, the captain directed Mogg to release the windmill arms. As the windmill creaked to a start, the generator began humming.

And inside the lantern, the light began to glow.

CHAPTER TEN

The light from the new lantern cast a strong beam out over the bay, making it easy for Sam and the children to return to Moonhaven. They had left Captain Luna behind, tending to his ship with Mogg's help.

"Mogg is very handy to have around—when he's on your side," Sam pointed out.

They had offered to help too, but the captain had sent them on their way.

"You've taken up enough of my time already" was the last thing he said, though he didn't look entirely unfriendly as he said it.

Videlia Potts was waiting for them at the dock. The air smelled faintly of onion soup.

"Glad to see you all in one piece, my dears," she said. "I expect you'll want to be getting home directly."

"I guess," said Michael. He had to admit that he liked it here in the Great Kettles even if everything

wasn't as scientific as it should be.

Sarah didn't want to leave either. There was so much they hadn't seen yet.

Joey frowned. "Do we have to go?" he asked.

"I'm afraid so," said Sam. "And no arguments, please."

He led the way back to the empty toy shop. The magic door was open inside, just as they had left it.

"Come back soon," Videlia said. "Especially you, Sam. Your shop needs a good cleaning."

"Your shop?" said Sarah.

Michael and Joey just stared.

Sam smiled. Long before, he had been the Sandman's apprentice, repairing the toys that children broke in their dreams. Eventually, he had opened this toy shop. But Sam decided he wanted to make toys for all children, so one day he had left the Kettles for the Outland.

"That's a story for another time," he said, running his hand gently along the counter. "Now, hurry along."

The Onion Lady gave them each a hug and watched as they walked through the doorway. Once they were on the other side, the magic door closed with a distinct *clank* behind them.

"Well, we're home!" cried Joey.

Just out of curiosity, Sarah turned back for one last look at the Kettles. But the door was locked and would not open.

The others glanced quickly around Sam's shop. The toys were still on the shelves. Sam's tools remained scattered over his workbench. Everything looked the same.

Michael sighed. "There's still a lot to clean up here."

"At least we don't have to worry about Mogg stomping around anymore," said Sarah.

"That's true," said Sam. "I suspect Mogg will stay pretty busy taking care of his new lighthouse. He won't have as much time to get into mischief. And I believe Videlia will invite him over for soup now and then."

"How are we going to explain being gone so long?" asked Sarah. "I'm going to be in big trouble. And it won't help if I tell my parents that I met a giant who had stolen the moon."

Michael looked at the mantel. "But, but, that's not possible! According to Sam's clock, we've only been gone twenty minutes."

"It is hard to understand," said Sam. "I gave up trying long ago. Time moves slower here than it does in Great Kettles."

"I wish I could use that trick when I do homework," said Sarah. "Hey, Joey, why the long face? Aren't you happy with the way things turned out?"

"I guess."

Joey looked out the window. There, just above the horizon, the moon was rising. It was a full moon, but there was a dark spot just below the middle.

"It looks like the captain didn't have time to replace the generator before sailing," said Michael. "But he was pretty pressed for time."

Joey sighed.

"So what's still bothering you?" Sarah asked.

"I was wondering if we'll ever be able to go back to the Great Kettles?"

Sarah and Michael turned to Sam with a million questions, but he only looked up at the moon and smiled.

"Only time will tell," he said.